Diggers are big — but elephants bigger.
If you want to shift mud and dig big holes,
best NOT let an elephant near the controls.

Don't let a **polar bear** cut your **hair** . . .

Unless, that is, you want people to stare.
She'll paw you and claw you and grab your hair tight.
Then snippety-snip — oh dear, what a fright!

Never be **woken** by a slithery **snake**...

YAWN

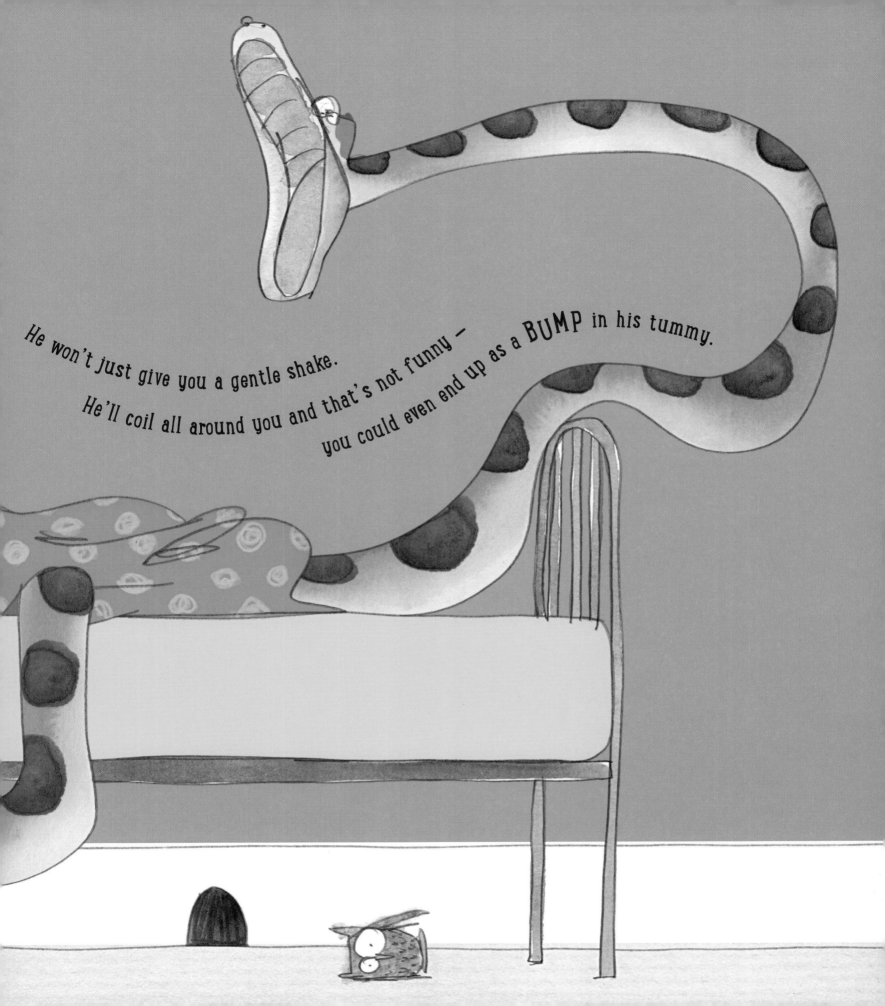

He won't just give you a gentle shake.
He'll coil all around you and that's not funny –
you could even end up as a BUMP in his tummy.

Don't join a **gorilla** for a **scooter** ride . . .

You'll **wobble** and **slip**,

swivel

and

slide.

But he'll just beat his chest and go **faster**.
Be warned – this scoot could end in disaster!

To let a **shark bath** you is a silly idea . . .

The sight of her jaws will fill you with fear.

And if she should offer to wash your back,
jump out QUICK –
she's about to
attack!

Never let a **seal** prepare you a **meal** . . .

Especially breakfast — you'll get a raw deal.
Of course, there is nothing wrong with fish.
But who wants a whole shoal in their dish?

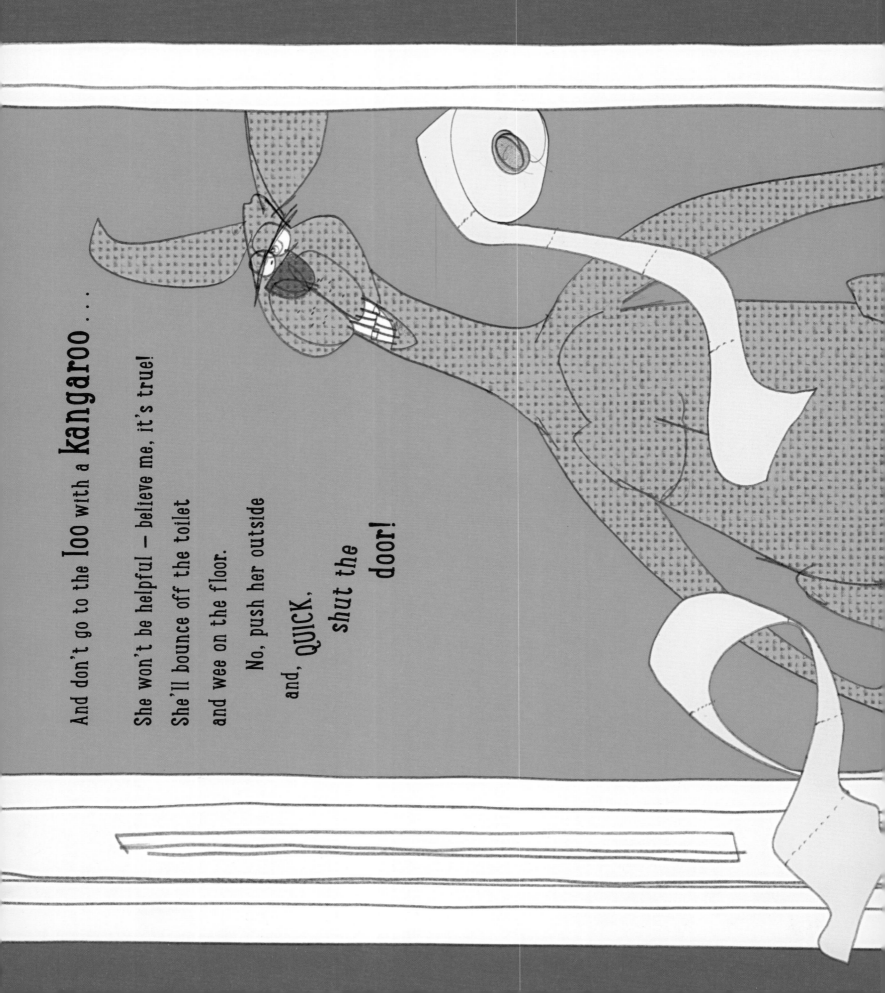

And don't go to the loo with a **kangaroo** . . . .

She won't be helpful – believe me, it's true!
She'll bounce off the toilet
and wee on the floor.
  No, push her outside
  and, QUICK,
    shut the
      door!

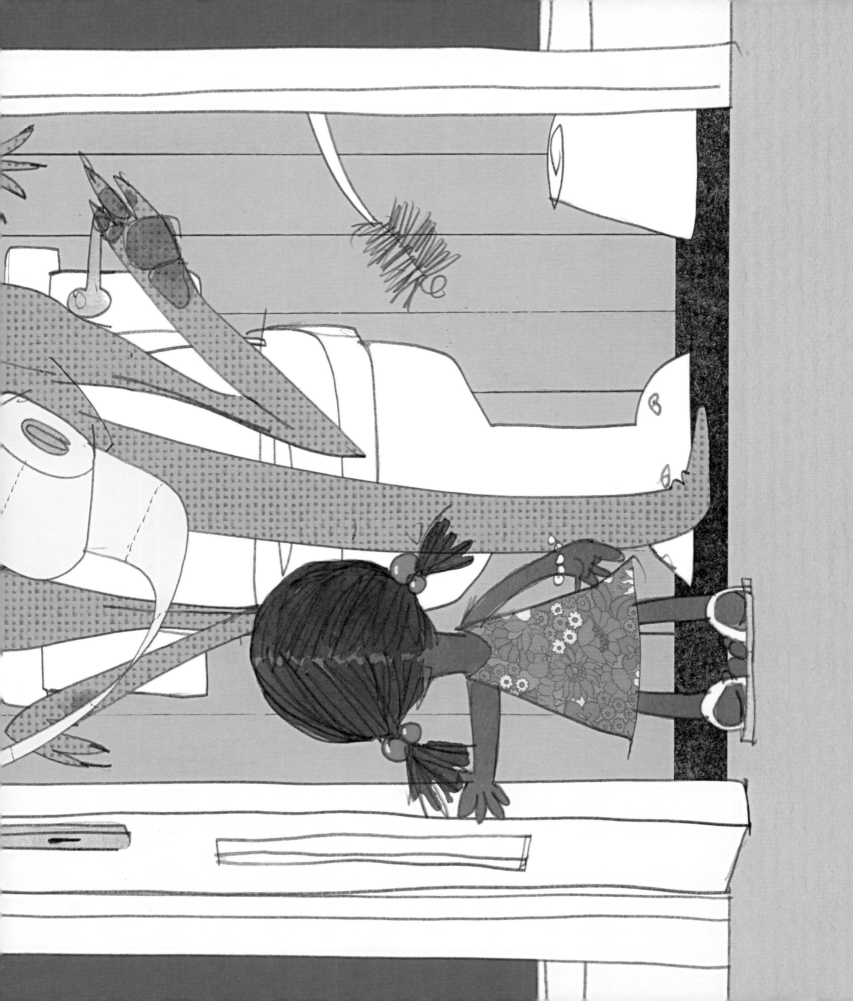

Nor should an **octopus** help you get **dressed** . . .

She'll have fun but you won't look your best.
With socks on your hands and pants for a hat —
you won't want to go out looking like THAT!

Never **brush your teeth** with a **crocodile** . . .

If he offers to help you — just run a mile.
He'll bite your toothbrush
and break it
in two.

And if he gets hungry — his snack could be YOU!

COOKING WITH KIDS

Don't let a **wolf** read your **bedtime story** . . .

He'll choose a tale both gruesome and gory.
And his eerie howling will drive you mad.
No, better leave story time to your dad.

Never – never EVER – share
a **skunk's** bunk . . .

He'll feast at midnight
on grubs, worms and junk.
Then, from his bottom,
he'll let out a **stink**
so vile and so nasty
you WON'T sleep
a wink.

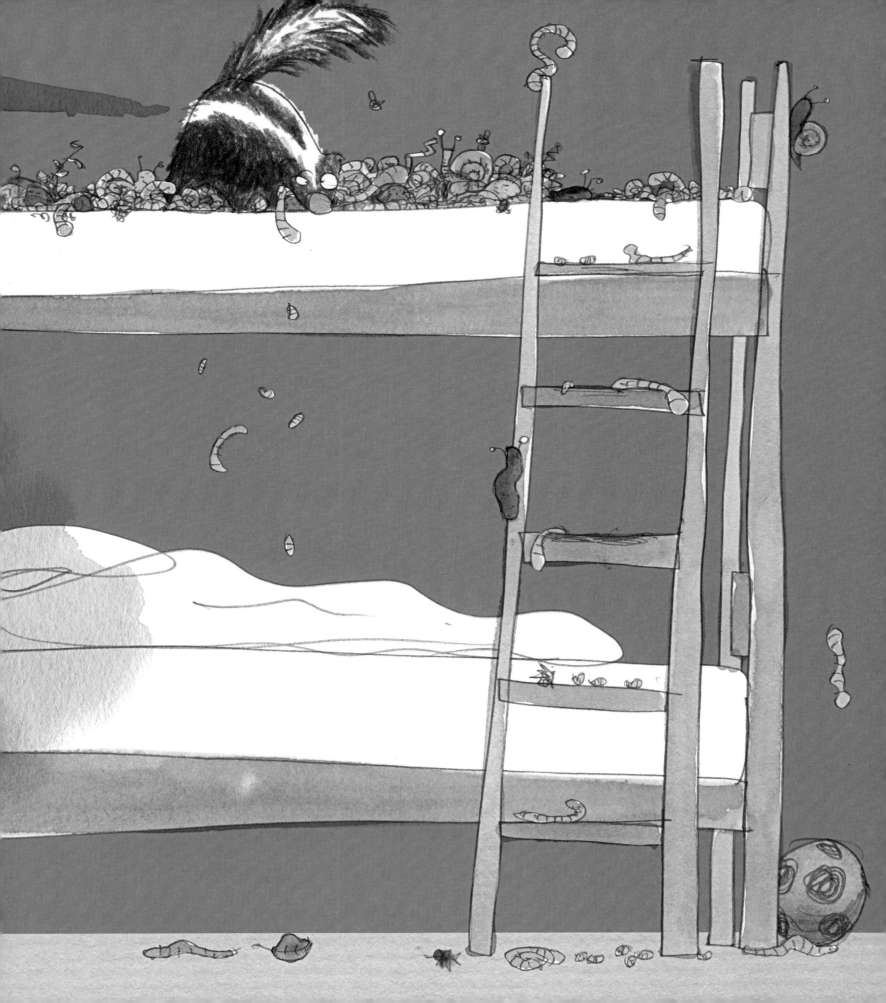

Well, here's an idea . . .

What do **you** say?

Forget about helping.

Let's just go and . . .

For James Catchpole, agent extraordinaire — PC-P

For Magic Starsmore — DT

BLOOMSBURY CHILDREN'S BOOKS
Bloomsbury Publishing Plc
50 Bedford Square, London, WC1B 3DP, UK
BLOOMSBURY, BLOOMSBURY CHILDREN'S BOOKS and the Diana logo are trademarks of Bloomsbury Publishing Plc
First published in Great Britain by Bloomsbury Publishing Plc

Text copyright © Patricia Cleveland-Peck 2018
Illustrations copyright © David Tazzyman 2018

Patricia Cleveland-Peck and David Tazzyman have asserted their rights under the Copyright, Designs and Patents Act, 1988,
to be identified as the Author and Illustrator of this work

A catalogue record for this book is available from the British Library

ISBN 978 1 4088 7913 9 (HB)
ISBN 978 1 4088 7914 6 (PB)
ISBN 978 1 4088 7915 3 (eBook)

1 3 5 7 9 10 8 6 4 2

Printed and bound in China by Leo Paper Products, Heshan, Guangdong
All papers used by Bloomsbury Publishing Plc are natural, recyclable products from wood grown in well managed forests.
The manufacturing processes conform to the environmental regulations of the country of origin.

To find out more about our authors and books visit www.bloomsbury.com and sign up for our newsletters